Mr. and Mrs. Button's Wonderful Watchdogs

Mr. and Mrs. Button's Wonderful Watchdogs

by JANICE

illustrated by ROGER DUVOISIN

Lothrop, Lee & Shepard Company, New York
A Division of William Morrow Co., Inc.

Library of Congress Catalog Card Number 78-8451
ISBN 0-688-41848-1   ISBN 0-688-51848-6 lib. bdg.
Printed in the United States of America.
First Edition   1 2 3 4 5 6 7 8 9 10

On a sunny slope, surrounded by flower gardens, stood the Button house. Every morning Mrs. Button called, "Breakfast, everybody," and everybody came running.

First came Sylvia, a brown and black dachshund. Then came Sunflower, a redheaded Persian cat, then Sadie, a plain alley cat with a pink nose and a gray patch over one eye. Last of all came Mr. Button.

One morning at breakfast Mr. Button said, "There's been another robbery in the village."

"Oh dear," said Mrs. Button. "If only Sylvia were a watchdog. She turned to Sylvia, "You silly dog. If a burglar came, you would only cover him with kisses."

"Arf, arf!" Sylvia agreed, barking joyfully.

"And you are no better," Mr. Button told the cats. "You have no pride. You ask every stranger who comes here to tickle your chins."

Sadie yawned. Sunflower was busy licking Mr. Button's plate clean.

"What we need is a real watchdog," said Mr.
Button.

So they went to the Watchdog Kennels
and said, "We want a watchdog to protect us
from burglars."

"You have come to the right place," said the
Kennel Keeper, and a fierce boxer was led out.

"Savage, show us how you scare a burglar," said the Kennel Keeper.

Savage leaped high off the ground, his front paws clawing the air. He growled angrily and looked ready to tear any burglar to pieces.

"Perfect," said Mr. Button.

"I feel safer already," said Mrs. Button.

Early the next morning Savage heard a burglar and rushed out of the house. The burglar was coming up the driveway with a wire basket filled with white bottles. Savage leaped into the air and growled, "Grrrrrr!"

The burglar dropped his basket, and the bottles broke.

Sylvia came running out to see why Savage was barking so fiercely. When she saw her friend the milkman, she ran over to him, jumped up, and licked his chin. Meanwhile, the milk came flowing down the driveway.

Then the cats came running out.

"Meow," Sunflower lifted her chin so the milk-man could tickle it.

Sadie sprang up onto his shoulder, twined herself around his neck, and purred.

Savage was so surprised he stopped barking. "Why are you so loving with this burglar?" he snarled.

Sylvia stared at him. "That's not a burglar, silly, that's a friend."

Savage was embarrassed. He saw he had made a mistake.

The same thing happened the next day when
another burglar drove up to the door. Almost every
day a burglar came but, when Savage tried to
do his duty as a watchdog, the burglar turned out
to be a friend.

Savage was all mixed up. He brooded over it. At
the end of a week he decided to change his ways.
When the next burglar came, he began to dance
around him and lick his hands, cheeks, and nose
just like the others.

"Some watchdog you turned out to be!" said
Mrs. Button. "You ought to be ashamed of
yourself!"

But Savage only jumped into her lap and licked
her ears.

So Mr. and Mrs. Button went to Howling Dog Kennels. This time they came home with Fury, a mean-looking German police dog.

The very next morning Fury was on the job. When a burglar arrived with a large parcel, Fury bared her teeth and leaped at his face. "Don't you dare come here, you burglar, or I'll eat you alive!" she growled.

The burglar was frightened. The parcel fell out of his hand and opened as it hit the ground.

Sylvia and Savage came running out. They crowded around their friend the laundry man, barking with pleasure. The cats came out and rubbed against his legs. The driveway was strewn with Mr. Button's shirts and Mrs. Button's nightgowns.

Fury couldn't believe her eyes. She was furious. "I'm trying to protect this house from burglars, and what do you do?"

The others only made fun of her. "That's not a burglar, silly, that's a friend."

Fury thought this over. "How do you know a burglar from a friend?" she asked.

"Everybody who comes here is a friend," said Sylvia and Savage.

"That's not what they told me at the Kennels," said Fury. But soon she, too, got used to the way burglars turned into friends in this strange house.

And Mr. and Mrs. Button decided to try the
Ferocious Dog Kennels.

This time they came home with Fire Eater, a
black Doberman Pinscher.

Fire Eater just hated burglars so, the next morn-
ing, when a burglar arrived with a basket of eggs,
Fire Eater got very angry. "Thief! Crook! Burglar!
I hate you! I'll chew you to pieces!"

The basket dropped out of the burglar's hand.
The eggs came spilling out. There were broken
eggshells and smashed egg yolks all over the
driveway.

Sylvia, Savage, Fury, and the cats came running. When they saw their dear friend the egg woman, they rushed over to her. The dogs barked and wagged their tails. The cats purred.

Fire Eater was surprised. He stopped barking at the burglar. "Is *that* the way to act when a burglar comes?" he barked angrily, standing watch over the broken eggs.

"That's not a burglar!" said Sylvia, Savage, and Fury. "That's the egg woman."

"They never said anything about an egg woman at the Kennels. They must have forgotten to tell me." Soon Fire Eater, too, gave up, and Mr. and Mrs. Button went to the Bare Fang Kennels.

This time they came home with the largest and

most fearful dog of all. He was an Irish wolfhound called Monster.

"Monster looks fierce enough and large enough to scare ten burglars. Now I'm sure we'll be well-protected," said Mrs. Button.

But she was wrong. Monster didn't want to catch burglars at all. He wanted to love somebody. Anybody. So first he loved Mr. and Mrs. Button. Next he began to love Sylvia, Savage, Fury, and Fire Eater. After that he fell in love with Sunflower. But, best of all, he loved Sadie, because she was so plain.

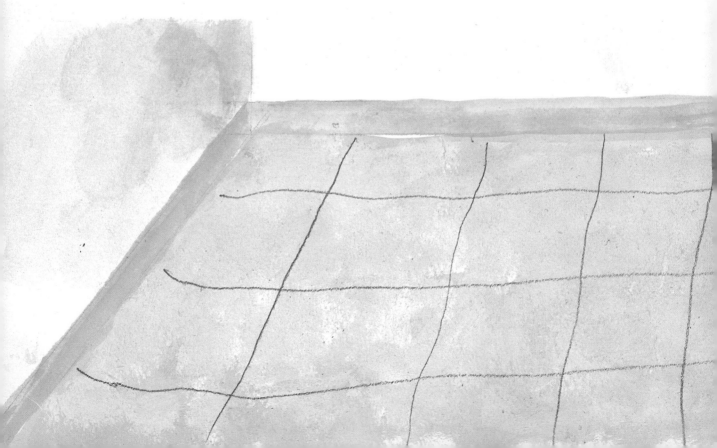

A week after Monster's arrival—guess who came?

THE BURGLAR!

It was late at night. He didn't make a sound as he came down the driveway. He didn't make a sound as he opened the kitchen door. "Fine," said the Burglar. "No dogs, no burglar alarm."

All the dogs lifted their heads and sniffed. The cats sniffed too—their ears wiggled with excitement.

"I smell another friend," barked Monster. And he hurled himself at the Burglar. So did Sylvia, Savage, Fury, and Fire Eater. So did Sadie and Sunflower.

The Burglar didn't know what was happening to him. Sadie climbed up onto one of his shoulders, purring. Sylvia pushed Monster aside so she could lick the Burglar's face. Savage pulled playfully at the Burglar's pants until they came undone and fell to his ankles. Sunflower tugged at the Burglar's shoe laces until they came untied. Fire Eater and Fury ran around him in circles. Monster pushed him lovingly against the cupboard.

The cupboard came crashing down. The drawers and doors flew open. The silver and dishes came pouring out.

"Help! Help!" cried the Burglar.

Mr. and Mrs. Button woke up. "There's a burglar in the house!" yelled Mr. Button.

"Help! Help!" screamed Mrs. Button.

When they ran downstairs, they found the frightened Burglar lying on the floor. Sylvia, Savage, Fury, Fire Eater, Monster, Sadie and Sunflower were rolling all over him, and licking him affectionately.

Mr. and Mrs. Button laughed so hard they didn't even think of calling the police.

The Burglar succeeded at last in freeing himself from all the dogs and cats. He tore out the door and RAN.

But Sylvia, Savage, Fury, Fire Eater, and Mon-

ster ran after him, barking, "Come back! Come back!"

Sadie and Sunflower followed behind purring, "We love you! We love you!"

"Look at this," said Mrs. Button, holding up the Burglar's shoes.

"And this," said Mr. Button, holding up the Burglar's pants.

"He'll catch a cold," said Mrs. Button, giggling.

"No he won't. It's a warm night," said Mr. Button, holding his sides.

"Anyway, no burglar will ever try to burgle this house again," said Mrs. Button.

"Not with our wonderful watchdogs to guard us," said Mr. Button.

"And our cats," added Mrs. Button.